The Fir Tree

HANS CHRISTIAN ANDERSEN

Illustrated by
SANNA ANNUKKA

Translated by
TIINA NUNNALLY

TEN SPEED PRESS
Berkeley

Published in the United States by Ten Speed Press,
an imprint of the Crown Publishing Group,
a division of Penguin Random House LLC, New York.
www.crownpublishing.com
www.tenspeed.com

Ten Speed Press and the Ten Speed Press colophon are
registered trademarks of Penguin Random House LLC.

This translation of 'The Fir Tree' first appeared in *Fairy Tales* by Hans
Christian Andersen, published by Penguin Classics, London, in 2004.

This illustrated edition was originally published in Great Britain by
Hutchinson, a Penguin Random House Company, London, in 2012.

Library of Congress Cataloging-in-Publication Data
Names: Andersen, H. C. (Hans Christian), 1805-1875. | Annukka, Sanna,
illustrator. | Nunnally, Tiina, 1952- translator. | Andersen, H. C. (Hans
Christian), 1805-1875. Tales. Selections. English.
Title: The fir tree / by Hans Christian Andersen ; illustrated by Sanna
Annukka ; translation by Tiina Nunnally.
Other titles: Grantrpet. English
Description: Berkeley, CA : Ten Speed Press, 2016. | "This translation of
'The Fir Tree' first appeared in Fairy Tales by Hans Christian Andersen,
published by Penguin Classics 2004"—Copyright page. | Originally
published in Great Britain by Hutchinson in 2012. | Summary: A little fir
tree realizes too late that it did not appreciate the grand moments of life,
such as being a Christmas tree, while they were happening.
Identifiers: LCCN 2015050251 |
Subjects: | CYAC: Fairy tales. | Christmas—Fiction.
| BISAC: FICTION / Fairy Tales, Folk Tales, Legends & Mythology.
| ART / Popular Culture. | FICTION / Classics.
Classification: LCC PZ8.A542 Fi 2016 | DDC [Fic]—dc23
LC record available at https://lccn.loc.gov/2015050251

Hardcover ISBN: 978-0-399-57848-9
eBook ISBN: 978-0-399-57849-6

Printed in China

Design by Jasper Goodall
Typeset by carrdesignstudio.com

10 9 8 7 6 5 4 3 2 1

First American Edition, 2016

for

Lukas & Lili

Out in the forest stood such a charming fir tree. It was in a good spot where it could get sunshine and there was plenty of air. All around grew scores of bigger companions, both firs and pines, but the little fir tree was so eager to grow up that it didn't think about the warm sun or the fresh air. It didn't pay any attention to the farm children who walked past, chattering, whenever they were out gathering strawberries or raspberries. Often they would come by with a whole pitcherful or they would have strawberries threaded on a piece of straw. Then they would sit down near the little tree and say, 'Oh, how charming and little it is!' That's not at all what the tree wanted to hear.

he following year it was a full length taller, and the year after that yet another. On a fir tree you can always tell how many years it has been growing by how many layers of branches it has.

'Oh, if only I were a big tree like the others,' sighed the little tree. 'Then I could spread out my branches all around and from the top I could gaze out on the wide world. The birds would build nests in my branches, and when the wind blew, I could nod so grandly, like all the others.'

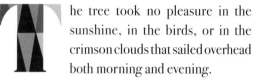he tree took no pleasure in the sunshine, in the birds, or in the crimson clouds that sailed overhead both morning and evening.

When it was winter, and the snow lay all around, glittering white, a hare often came bounding along and sprang right over the little tree. Oh, how annoying that was! But two winters passed and by the third the tree was so tall that the hare had to go around it. 'Oh, to grow and grow, to get bigger and older. That is the only lovely thing in this world,' thought the tree.

In the autumn the woodcutters would always appear to chop down some of the biggest trees. It happened every year, and the young fir tree, which was now quite grown-up, would start trembling because the tall, magnificent trees would topple to the ground with a groan and a crash. Their branches would be cut off, and they looked so naked, tall and slender. They were almost beyond recognition. But then they were loaded onto wagons, and horses carried them away, out of the forest.

here were they going? What was in store for them?

In the spring, when the swallow and stork appeared, the tree asked them: 'Do you know where they were taken? Have you seen them?'

The swallows didn't know anything, but the stork looked thoughtful, nodded his head, and said, 'Oh, yes, I think so. I met many new ships as I flew here from Egypt. On the ships were magnificent mast trees, and I'd venture to say they were yours. They smelled of fir. I bring you many greetings. How they swaggered and swayed!'

'Oh, if only I too were big enough to fly across the sea! What is the sea like, anyway? How does it look?'

'Well, it's much too complicated to describe,' said the stork and flew off.

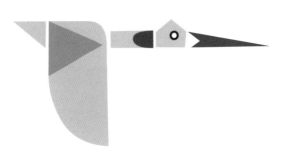

'Enjoy your youth!' said the rays of sunlight. 'Enjoy your fresh growth and the young life inside you!'

The wind kissed the tree, and the dew shed tears over it, but the fir tree did not understand.

hen Christmastime came, quite young trees were felled, trees that were often not even as tall or as old as the fir tree, which could never find any peace but was always eager to be off. These young trees, and they were the most beautiful of all, always kept their branches. They were loaded onto wagons, and horses carried them away, out of the forest.

'Where are they going?' asked the fir tree. 'They're no bigger than I am. There was even one that was much smaller. Why do they keep all their branches? Where are they being taken?'

'We know! We know!' chirped the sparrows. 'In town we've looked in the windows. We know where they're being taken. Oh, they end up in the greatest splendour and glory you could ever imagine. We've looked in the windows and seen them being planted in the middle of the warm parlour and decorated with the loveliest things: gilded apples, gingerbread, toys, and hundreds of candles!'

'And then?' asked the fir tree, all its branches aquiver. 'And then? What happens next?'

'Well, that's all we saw. But nothing could match it.'

'Maybe I was meant to take this glorious path,' rejoiced the fir tree. 'That's even better than going across the sea. What an agony of longing! If only it were Christmas. Now I'm as tall and broad as the others that were carried off last year. Oh, if only I were on that wagon right now. If only I were in the warm parlour with all that splendour and glory! And then . . . ? Well, then something even better is bound to happen, something even more wonderful, or why would they decorate me like that? Something even grander, even more glorious is bound to happen. But what? Oh, how I'm suffering! Oh, how I yearn! I just don't know what's come over me.'

'Take pleasure in us!' said the air and the sunlight. 'Take pleasure in your fresh youth out in the open!'

But the fir tree felt no pleasure at all. It grew and grew. Both winter and summer it was green; dark green it stood there. Everyone who saw it said, 'That's a lovely tree!' And at Christmas, it was the very first to be cut down. The axe bit deep into its marrow, and the tree fell to the ground with a sigh. It felt a pain, a weakness, it couldn't even think about happiness. It was sad to part with its home, with the spot where it had sprouted up, for the tree realised that it would never see its dear old companions again: the small shrubs and flowers all around, maybe not even the birds. Leaving was certainly not pleasant.

he tree didn't recover until it was unloaded in a courtyard with all the other trees and it heard a man say, 'That one is magnificent. That's the one we want.'

Then two servants in fine livery came and carried the fir tree into an enormous, beautiful room. Portraits hung on all the walls, and next to the large woodstove stood big Chinese vases with lions on the lids. There were rocking chairs, silk-covered sofas, big tables covered with picture books, and toys worth a hundred times a hundred *rigsdaler* – at least that's what the children said. And the fir tree was set in a large wooden tub filled with sand, but no one could tell that it was a wooden tub because green fabric was wrapped all around it, and the tub stood on top of a big, colourful carpet.

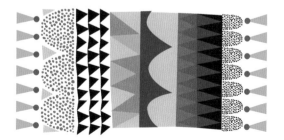

Oh, how the tree trembled! What was going to happen next? Then the servants and the maids proceeded to decorate the tree. On one branch they hung little woven baskets cut out of coloured paper; each basket was filled with sweets. Gilded apples and walnuts hung on the tree as if they had grown there, and more than a hundred little candles, red and blue and white, were fastened to the branches. Dolls that looked as lifelike as human beings swayed in the boughs. The tree had never seen anything like it before. And at the very top they put a big star made from shiny gold paper. It was magnificent, quite incomparably magnificent.

'Tonight,' they all said, 'tonight the tree will shine!'

'Oh,' thought the tree. 'If only it were evening. If only they'd light the candles soon. And what will happen after that? Will trees come from the forest to look at me? Will the sparrows fly past the window? Will I take root and stand here, decorated like this, all winter and summer long?'

Oh yes, the tree thought it knew all about it. But it had a terrible bark-ache from sheer yearning, and bark-aches are just as bad for trees as headaches are for the rest of us.

Finally the candles were lit. What splendour, what magnificence! Every branch of the tree trembled so much that one of the candles set fire to a bough. How it stung!

'God help us!' shrieked the maids, and hastily put out the fire.

Now the tree didn't even dare tremble. Oh, how awful! It was so afraid of losing any of its finery. It was quite bedazzled by all the splendour. And then the double doors flew open, and a crowd of children rushed in, as if they were about to topple the whole tree. The grownups followed more sedately. The children stood in utter silence, but only for a moment. Then they began shouting again so their voices echoed through the room. They danced around the tree, and one present after the other was plucked from the branches.

‘What are they doing?' thought the tree. ‘What's going to happen?' And the candles burned all the way down to the boughs, and as they burned down, they were put out, and then the children were allowed to plunder the tree. Oh, how they rushed at it, making all the branches groan. If the tree hadn't been tied to the ceiling by its top and the gold star, it would have toppled right over.

The children danced around with their splendid toys. No one paid any attention to the tree except for the old nursemaid, who walked around it, peering in among the branches. But she was only checking to see that not a fig or apple had been overlooked.

'A story! A story!' shouted the children, pulling a stout little man over to the tree, and he sat down right underneath it. 'Because we're out in the forest,' he told them, 'and it may do the tree some good to listen along! But I'm only going to tell you one story. Do you want to hear the one about Ickety-Ackety or the one about Clumpa-Dumpa, who fell down the stairs but still ended up on the throne and won the hand of the princess?'

'Ickety-Ackety!' cried some of the children. 'Clumpa-Dumpa!' cried the others.

They shouted and shrieked, and only the fir tree stood in silence and thought, 'Won't I get to take part? Won't I get to do anything?' It had been part of the celebration, after all; it had done what it was supposed to do.

And then the man told the story of Clumpa-Dumpa, who fell down the stairs but still ended up on the throne and won the hand of the princess. And the children clapped their hands and shouted, 'Tell us more, tell us more!' They wanted to hear the one about 'Ickety-Ackety' too, but he would only tell them the story about Clumpa-Dumpa. The fir tree stood quite still and pensive. The birds in the forest had never mentioned anything like this. 'Clumpa-Dumpa fell down the stairs, and yet won the hand of the princess. Well, well, so that's the way the things are out in the world,' thought the fir tree, believing that it was all true because such a nice man had told the story. 'Well, well! Who knows, maybe I too will fall down the stairs and win the princess.' And the fir tree looked forward to the next day when it would be adorned with candles and toys, gold and fruit.

'Tomorrow I won't tremble,' it thought. 'I will fully enjoy all my glory. Tomorrow I'll hear the story about Clumpa-Dumpa again, and maybe the one about Ickety-Ackety too.' And the tree stood still and pensive all night long.

In the morning a servant and a maid came into the room.

'Now the finery is going to start again!' thought the tree. But they dragged it out of the parlour and up the stairs to the attic. And there, in a dark corner where no daylight shone, they left it. 'What does this mean?' thought the tree. 'I wonder what I'm supposed to do here? I wonder what I'm going to hear now?' It leaned against the wall and stood there thinking and thinking. And it had plenty of time for that, because day after day and night after night went by.

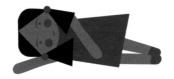

N o one came up to the attic, and when someone finally did, it was only to put some large boxes in the corner. The tree stood quite hidden; you would almost think it had been completely forgotten.

'Now it's winter outside,' thought the tree. 'The ground is hard and covered with snow. The people wouldn't be able to plant me. No doubt that's why I'm standing here, safe indoors until springtime. What a good plan! How kind the people are! If only it wasn't so dark in here and so terribly lonely. There's not even a little hare. It was so nice out there in the forest when the snow lay on the ground and the hare came running past. Yes, even when it leaped right over me, although I didn't like it much at the time. But up here it's terribly lonely.'

'queak, squeak!' said a little mouse at that very moment and came scurrying. And then another little mouse appeared. They sniffed at the fir tree and scurried in and out of its branches.

'It's awfully cold,' said the little mice. 'But otherwise it's quite blissful to be here. Don't you agree, you old fir tree?'

'I'm not old at all!' said the fir tree. 'There are plenty of trees that are much older than I am!'

'Where did you come from?' asked the mice. 'And what do you know?' They were awfully curious. 'Tell us about the loveliest place on earth! Have you ever been there? Have you been in the pantry where cheeses are lined up on the shelves and hams hang from the ceiling? Where you can dance on tallow candles? Where you go in skinny but come out fat?'

'I don't know that place,' said the tree. 'But I do know the forest, where the sun shines and the birds sing.' And then the tree told them all about its youth, and the young mice had never heard anything like that before. They listened closely and said, 'Oh, you've seen so much! How happy you've been!'

'Me?' said the fir tree, thinking about everything it had just described. 'Why yes, I suppose those were quite delightful days, after all.' But then the tree told them about Christmas Eve, when it was decorated with cakes and candles.

'Oh!' said the little mice. 'How happy you've been, you old fir tree!'

'I'm not old at all!' said the tree. 'It was only this winter that I came here from the forest. I'm in the prime of my life, I've just stopped growing.'

'How wonderfully you describe things!' said the little mice, and the following night they brought along four other little mice who wanted to hear what the tree had to tell. And the more the tree told them, the more clearly it remembered everything and thought, 'Those actually were quite enjoyable days. But they can come again, they can come again! Clumpa-Dumpa fell down the stairs, yet he won the hand of the princess. Maybe I too can win a princess.' And then the fir tree thought about a charming little birch tree that grew out in the forest. For the fir tree, the birch was a real and lovely princess.

'Who's Clumpa-Dumpa?' asked the little mice. And then the fir tree told them the whole story; it could remember every single word. And the little mice were ready to run all the way to the top of the tree out of sheer glee. The next night many more mice came, and on Sunday there were even two rats. But they said the story wasn't amusing, and that made the little mice sad, because then they thought less of the story themselves.

'Is that the only story you know?' asked the rats.

'The only one,' replied the tree. 'I heard it on the happiest evening of my life, but back then I didn't realise how happy I was!'

'It's an exceptionally tedious story. Don't you know any about bacon and tallow candles? Any pantry stories?'

'No,' said the tree.

'Well, thanks for nothing!' replied the rats and they went back home.

Eventually the little mice disappeared too, and then the tree sighed, 'It was so nice having those nimble little mice sitting around me and listening to what I told them. Now that too is over. But I'm going to remember to enjoy myself when they finally take me out of here.'

But when would that happen?

Well, one day in the early morning, servants came up to the attic and started rummaging around. The boxes were moved aside, and the tree was pulled out. Now, it's true that they threw it to the floor rather hard, but then a man dragged it at once toward the stairs, where daylight was shining.

'Now life will begin again!' thought the tree. It could feel the fresh air, the first rays of sun. And then it was out in the courtyard. Everything happened so fast that the tree forgot all about taking a look at itself. There was so much to see all around. The courtyard was next to a garden, and everything was in bloom. The roses hung so fresh and fragrant over the little fence, the linden trees were blossoming, and the swallows flew about, saying, 'Kirra-virra-vit, my husband has arrived!' But it wasn't the fir tree they meant.

'Now I'm going to live!' rejoiced the tree, spreading its branches wide. But alas, its boughs were all withered and yellow. In the corner among the weeds and nettles was where the tree came to rest. The star made from gold paper was still on its top, shimmering in the bright sunshine.

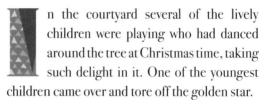n the courtyard several of the lively children were playing who had danced around the tree at Christmas time, taking such delight in it. One of the youngest children came over and tore off the golden star.

'Look what's still sitting on the horrid old Christmas tree!' he said, stomping on the branches so they groaned under his boots.

And the tree looked at all the floral splendour and freshness in the garden. Then it looked at itself and wished that it had stayed in the dark corner of the attic. The tree thought about its fresh youth in the forest, about the joyous Christmas Eve, and about the little mice who had listened so happily to the story about Clumpa-Dumpa.

'It's over, it's over!' said the poor tree. 'If only I had enjoyed it while I could. It's over, it's over!'

nd the hired man came over and chopped the tree into little pieces; it made a whole stack. How lovely the tree flared up under the big copper cauldron. And it sighed so deeply; each sigh was like the sound of a little shot. That's why the children who were playing came running over and sat down in front of the fire, staring into the flames and shouting, 'Bang, snap!' But with each sharp crack, which was a deep sigh, the tree thought about a summer day in the forest, or about a winter night out there, when the stars were shining. It thought about Christmas Eve and about Clumpa-Dumpa, the only story it had ever heard and knew how to tell. And before long the tree had burned up.

The boys played in the courtyard, and on his chest the youngest one had the gold star that the tree had worn on its happiest evening. Now it was over, and the tree was gone, along with the story. It was over, over, and that's what happens to every story!

The
End

HANS CHRISTIAN ANDERSEN was born in
Odense, Denmark, in 1805. The son of a cobbler
and a washerwoman, he didn't start school until
he was seventeen. He became famous for his fairy
tales, including classics such as *The Ugly Duckling*
and *The Snow Queen*. *The Fir Tree* was published
in 1845. When he died aged 70, the king and crown
prince of Denmark attended his funeral.

SANNA ANNUKKA spent her childhood summers
in Finland, and its landscape and folklore remain a
source of inspiration.

A print maker and illustrator based in Brighton,
she is also a designer for Finnish textile brand
Marimekko and has been featured in *Vogue* and
many interior design magazines. *The Fir Tree* is her
first book.